DATE DUE		
DEC 02 1991		
OCT 20 1997		
GAYLORD No. 2333		PRINTED IN U.S.A.

Fox in a Trap

Also by Jane Resh Thomas

Elizabeth Catches a Fish
The Comeback Dog
Courage at Indian Deep
Wheels

Fox in a Trap

by Jane Resh Thomas

Drawings by Troy Howell

Clarion Books

TICKNOR & FIELDS: A HOUGHTON MIFFLIN COMPANY

New York

Clarion Books
Ticknor & Fields, a Houghton Mifflin Company
Text copyright © 1987 by Jane Resh Thomas
Illustrations copyright © 1987 by Troy Howell

Library of Congress Cataloging-in-Publication Data

Thomas, Jane Resh.
Fox in a trap.
Summary: Daniel looks forward to helping his Uncle
Peter set traps for the foxes that have been plaguing
the family farm, until the discovery of a severed fox
paw makes him seriously question what he and his uncle
are doing.
[1. Trapping—Fiction. 2. Foxes—Fiction.
3. Animals—Treatment—Fiction. 4. Country life—
Fiction] I. Howell, Troy, ill. II. Title.
PZ7.T36695Fo 1987   [Fic]   86-17412
ISBN 0-89919-473-7

V 10 9 8 7 6 5 4 3 2

For *Judith Markham Beckman and Richard Resh*

Ports in a storm,
Breezes in a calm.

J.R.T.

Fox in a Trap

One

A cow trudged up to the watering tank where Daniel stood. Her tail flapped against her sides, raising a buzz of flies with every stroke. When she grazed Daniel's back with the dirty tassel on the end of her tail, he moved a few steps down the side of the tank without looking up. His hands still cupped around his eyes, he looked through his own shadow into the deep, dark water.

There among the flowing strands of green algae, he saw an orange flash, one of the goldfish that Uncle Pete had given him. "A taste of the tropics," his uncle had said. "A mind trip off the farm."

"Pete," Pa had said quietly, "Daniel's mind is off the farm half the time now. He has trouble enough remembering to feed the chickens, without adding tropical livestock."

Daniel had fed the fish faithfully and kept their water clean, partly to prove that Pa was wrong about him. In the spring, when even Uncle Pete's fancy aquarium seemed too much like a prison, Daniel had set the pair of goldfish free in the cattle trough. He looked for them every day to make sure they were still alive.

"They'll freeze out next winter," his father said now, handing Daniel a bucket of chicken feed. "And they'll grow too big in that tank to fit the bowl next fall."

Daniel noticed that Pa refused to use Uncle Pete's word, *aquarium*. "I'll figure what to do when fall comes," he said.

As he carried the heavy bucket to the chicken yard, he looked around for his dog. Every time he thought of Lady, his stomach flipped. She might have run away again, now that her sore feet were beginning to heal. She had come back only a few days ago, with her feet cut up and her muzzle bristling with porcupine quills, a half-starved scarecrow.

Daniel caught sight of her as he scattered a handful of chicken feed and poured the rest into the feeder. She limped stiffly around the rockpile at the edge of the field, sniffing the air and nosing between the rocks. She needed a cane, Daniel thought.

He laughed when a chipmunk darted out of the rocks, flicked its tail, and chucked at the dog. Lady growled a low *woof* and pranced around the rocks as fast as her limp would let her. The chipmunk disappeared when Pa rumbled past on the tractor, headed for the field with a load of seed corn for planting.

"It's a beautiful circle," Pa always told Daniel in the springtime. "The cow manure fertilizes the corn. The cows eat the corn. Then their manure fertilizes another crop."

Ignoring the noise of the tractor, the empty-headed chickens rushed for the mash at Daniel's feet, pecking the ground, pecking one another, pecking little stones between their scrawny toes. But Daniel shut them out of his thoughts as he read the letter from Uncle Pete again.

He had carried it in the hip pocket of his jeans until the envelope was ragged. He touched the return address, Anchorage, Alaska, with his fingers, as if to absorb faraway places through his skin.

"Dear Dan," the letter said. "You talked me into it. Next winter I'll show you how to use those traps you found in the barn, if you'll promise to do more than your share of the work. I learned some tricks from Alaskan trappers this winter. Love, Uncle Pete. P.S. You might not go for trapping when you see how mean it is."

Daniel was determined to show Uncle Pete that he wasn't a baby anymore, a little kid who would faint at the sight of blood. He planned to help Pa with the butchering next time. Certainly he was old enough to be Uncle Pete's trapping partner.

Daniel turned his gaze to Lady. She won't run away today, he thought, not with that limp. Still he worried. What about tomorrow and the day after that? He recalled the cold morning he had found her almost dead in the ditch. He had fed her. He had brought her back from the dead, when nobody else believed she'd live through the night.

I was grown up enough for that, he thought. He remembered how he'd taken her for a walk by the creek when she'd seemed strong enough. He saw her again, bolting for the woods, disappearing into the brush. And again he imagined her lying in a wedge of sunlight in the barn, come back of her own free will, her infected nose looking like a pincushion, her feet cut and bleeding.

Now she chased the agile chipmunk on the shady side of the rocks. Even though she might run away again, there would be no leashes and choke collars this time, Daniel had decided; she would stay because she wanted to, or she wouldn't stay at all.

Lady suddenly began to bark, a wild note in her voice. Daniel rushed to see what was the matter. He heard a high buzzing, not the sound of a bumblebee nor of a fly caught between windowpanes, but a higher pitched, softer, drier whir. It was the sound of a hiss married to the sustained rustling of fallen leaves.

Daniel's heart thudded in his chest. He had heard that sound before, in the field near the creek, last summer when Pa had killed a rattlesnake with a shovel.

"Lady!" he shouted in a panic. Growling and barking wildly, the dog rushed the snake and then leapt back. Daniel grabbed her around the neck. "Mama!"

As Daniel clutched the dog's silky fur and dragged her back from the rocks, the screen door slammed.

"Get the shovel!" Daniel shouted so loud his voice broke and squeaked. "Mama! The shovel!"

Then he saw the snake. It was not neatly coiled, as people imagine rattlesnakes are when they prepare to strike. Instead it lay in a sharply curved S on the sand, its rattling tail erect, its head reared back. It was bobbing and weaving like a muscular boxer luring an adversary into a foolish mistake.

Lady struggled in Daniel's grip, trying to charge the snake. Mama strode across the yard in a few long steps, a shovel in one hand.

"We'll fix his wagon," she said in her calm way. "Hang on to that dog."

Holding the shovel handle between her outstretched hands, she walked deliberately up to the snake. It swayed back and forth, trying to get into striking range of Mama's ankles. Daniel thought his heart would leap clear out of his chest, it was beating so hard.

But Mama stood her ground. When the snake gath-

ered itself for an instant, she plunged the shovel straight down. The snake lashed back, and Daniel thought it would strike again, but it coiled and writhed upon itself like a living knot. Mama dropped her hands to her sides. The shovel stood at attention by itself, its blade driven six inches into the dirt. Daniel saw that the snake's head lay on one side of the shovel, while its knotted body squirmed on the other.

Still restraining Lady as Mama had instructed him, Daniel stared at her, speechless and heavy with the shock of what had happened. Mama's face glistened. Droplets of sweat coursed down her cheek and under her collar.

She wiped her face and neck with her apron. "Well, I'm glad that's over. I think I'll just sit here and catch my breath."

Trembling, she sat down in her tracks. She reached for Daniel and pulled him down in the sand with her. "You can let Lady go now."

She tried to hug Daniel, but he was on his knees, looking over her shoulder at the snake's triangular severed head. It was like a magnet for his eyes. He couldn't look away from it.

"That snake tried to bite you," said Daniel, "but you just stood right there."

"Well, he's only a little thing," Mama said. "It isn't as if he was a python or a diamondback. These massasauga rattlesnakes we grow in Michigan don't amount to much."

But her hands still trembled, Daniel noticed. "*Shoom!*" he said, plunging an imaginary shovel into the ground. "You just stood there and killed the thing!"

The tortured movement of the snake's body had subsided now, although it still twitched slightly in the dust. Lady growled, cautiously rushing it and then dodging away, her lips curled back from her teeth.

Daniel wrenched the shovel out of the ground and picked up the snake head on its blade. "Look at that," he said. "It's no bigger than a chicken head. He seemed as big as a dragon."

"They're not much worse than a nest of hornets," said Mama. Daniel started to sit down on the rocks.

"Get away from there!" she said, standing up. "Where there's one, there are probably more, and they must be nesting in those rocks."

She thought a moment. "They are worse than hornets, Daniel, but not as bad as diamondbacks. Did you know your grandpa used to eat diamondbacks when he lived out west?" Daniel clutched his throat and made a poisoned face. "Said they tasted like greasy chicken."

Standing on the snake's body with one foot, Daniel straightened it out with the other. "Thirty inches long, I'd say. Big enough to reach above boots. Even if you had been wearing them." He looked at Mama's ankles, delicate and bony under thin white socks. "Pa said you should always wear boots when you go after snakes."

She shuddered. "There wasn't time."

"Can we skin him and tack him on the barn for a trophy?"

"I don't much like trophies, Daniel."

"It's only a rattlesnake."

"Not even rattlesnakes for trophies. Who wants a snakeskin staring him in the face first thing every morning anyway?" She smiled. "Now, the Indians . . ." she went on, "the Indians thought that all creatures are brothers."

"Not me and rattlesnakes. Not wolf spiders," said Daniel. "Deer, maybe. Dogs, for sure."

"Oh, you want to pick the vegetarians and the helpers for brothers, do you?" Mama said. "You can take the rattle, if you want it. Put it with the others."

Holding down the snake's body with one foot, Daniel cut the rattle off the tail with his pocketknife. He would put it in his box of treasures with the rattles from the six other snakes his family had killed on the farm.

He counted the segments as he held it in the palm of his hand. "Seven," he said. It looked like a narrow gray insect shell, invisibly jointed. He couldn't see what made the rattle work.

"Some people say there's a rattle for every year of the snake's life," his mother said. "I don't know."

Daniel shook the rattle as fast as he could, but he couldn't make it whir as the snake had. He put it in his jeans pocket.

"Look at Lady," he said. The dog was methodically pushing dirt over the rattlesnake's body. Soon it was buried entirely. "She can't stand the sight of that snake."

"Or else the smell."

"Neither can I," said Daniel.

He dug a deep hole and pushed the head in with his shoe. "I don't want to take any chances of stepping on those fangs barefoot someday," he said.

He fingered the rattle that had terrified him a few minutes before. I could have killed that snake by myself, he thought. He imagined the shovel in his own hands, beheading the snake and making that *shoom!* sound as he drove it into the sand.

Something cold in the palm of his other hand scared him out of his hero dreams. Mama smiled at the way he jumped. Lady was nuzzling his hand with her sandy nose, wagging her tail, looking for a scratch and a pat and maybe a word of praise.

Mama put her arm around Daniel. "You were brave," she said. "And you know, I think maybe Lady's decided to stay."

Two

After supper that night, Daniel and Pa walked out to the orchard, with Lady limping along behind.

"Show me your snake," said Pa when they came to the rockpile.

Daniel uncovered the snake with the toe of his shoe and picked it up on a stick. Lady snuffed and curled her lips.

"That's a good-size one," said Pa. "It was a mistake for us to dump these rocks so near the chicken coop. Rocks draw snakes, and snakes drool when they think of eggs."

"How will we know if there are more rattlesnakes in there?"

"We'll just have to watch out for them. Late next

fall, after the snakes lay up for the winter, we'll haul the rocks to Brenners' place. They're filling in that ravine. The snakes will be so sleepy then, they won't be dangerous."

Pa dropped the snake's body. "The crows will get this fellow," he said. Lady immediately began burying the snake again.

"I'm proud of you and Mama, Daniel," said Pa. "You're not quite ten, and already you're taking a man's part sometimes."

In the orchard, the peach trees were blooming. Lake Michigan softened the winters here, so peaches and other fruit trees thrived. Daniel and Pa stood smiling at each other among the trees, breathing deeply, as if to fill their bodies with the perfume of the blossoms. Even this close to sundown, the bees were still loud in the trees.

When a wayward gust of wind blew up, a cloud of pink petals fell, drifting on their shoulders and in their hair. They held their palms out, opened their mouths, and stuck out their tongues to catch the petals, as people do to welcome rain.

"It's raining flowers," Daniel whispered, as if this

beauty were all new to him, as if he had never seen
another spring.

Pa pulled a branch down. With the pearl-handled
jackknife that he carried in the bib of his overalls, he
cut a flower from the tree, as he did every year, and
held it aloft in the palm of his hand. As always, the
knife was razor-sharp. Pa cut the flower lengthwise.
The halves fell open on his hand, and Daniel saw the
swelling in the heart of the flower that would be the
peach.

His father said nothing as he touched the infant fruit with the point of the knife. Daniel was silent. But the little golden hairs on his arms stood up.

"I'm a brother to the trees," he said softly, looking into his father's eyes, half embarrassed, uncertain whether Pa would understand.

"And so am I," said Pa. He buried his face in a cluster of blossoms and breathed their perfume pure. Daniel did the same.

As they turned to go, Lady tipped her head this way and that, trying to follow the flight path of a bumblebee.

"Our few cows are all right," said Pa. "And I don't mind raising the corn they need. But this orchard, Daniel. I love this orchard."

Across the nursery, the plot where row after row of seedling trees were planted, Daniel saw the kitchen light in the window. Gold and pink lit the sky. The windmill squeaked in the breeze.

"Tell about clearing the land again, Pa."

"Grandpa and Uncle Pete and I cleared every acre of this farm ourselves when I was your age, and Pete was twenty," said Pa. "We worked with crosscut saws and double-bitted axes. We burned the brush, and the smoke choked us. We turned up whole families of rattlesnakes, with all their aunts and cousins, back by the creek where the cornfield is now. And all the while, I kept imagining the taste of peaches, and seeing the cherries on the branch. There were always orchards in my dreams. That's what got me through all the misery and the killing work."

Pa rubbed his chin. "Still does, as a matter of fact."

Satisfied that the old familiar story hadn't changed since he last heard it, Daniel whistled for Lady. She was lollygagging way behind.

"Look, Pa. She's got her head down that old fox-hole."

"That reminds me," said Pa. "Your mother and I had a letter from Uncle Pete. He says you two are going to set a trapline next winter."

"Do you mind?" said Daniel.

"I suppose not," said Pa. "There have been so many foxes the past couple of years, they've eaten most of the pheasants. Now they're breaking down the chicken coop doors like rustlers and carrying off whole flocks in pickup trucks. The FBI is offering a reward for information leading to their arrest and conviction."

Daniel laughed. "Oh, Pa. You're silly."

"That's why I'm so much fun."

"Be serious, Pa."

"On the whole, I'd rather not interfere with the foxes," said Pa, "as long as they don't interfere with me. Their overpopulation would level out naturally, if we gave it a couple of years."

He put his hand on Daniel's shoulder. "But if you're bound and determined to team up with Pete on some project, why, go ahead. But trapping isn't pretty. I don't think you're going to like it, Daniel."

"How do you know?" Daniel said. Pa looked at him sharply.

Daniel clammed up. But inside, his temper flared. *There you go again, treating me like a baby. You don't know everything about me, Pa. I'm nothing like you. I hate all the hard work!*

The thoughts he couldn't bring himself to say aloud rumbled in Daniel's heart like thunder. He knew that someday, as soon as he was old enough, he would leave this farm and go traveling, like Uncle Pete.

He watched Lady scratching at the foxhole, oblivious to Daniel. More than ever now, he longed for Captain, the old dog who had died last winter. Captain had been closer than his best friend, closer even than Daniel's father. Captain always understood. Now, Daniel thought, nobody did.

Three

Lady stayed near Daniel whatever he did. She was beside him when he gathered the eggs and fed the cows. And she was there when he cleaned the chicken coop one morning, with one eye on his work and the other watching the road for Uncle Pete's car. Lady dozed in the yard, ignoring the hens, still tired from her weeks on the run. A chicken pecked a fly that was crawling on her leg, but she hardly flinched.

All the same, Daniel thought he needed eyes in the back of his head to keep track of the dog. Despite Mama's confidence that Lady would stay now, fear that she might run away again had become a habit with him. She was always there when he looked, but she was like a shadow, a watcher at the edge of things.

As Daniel shoveled the chicken droppings toward the door of the coop, he heard Uncle Pete's car horn tooting the first five notes of the old song, "Let Me Call You Sweetheart." He dropped the shovel on the chicken coop floor and ran to catch up with the car as Uncle Pete pulled it in under the oak to protect its green finish from the sun.

Daniel wanted to sit in the leather driver's seat and put down the top and feel the polished wood of the steering wheel in his hands. He wanted Uncle Pete to take him for a ride and maybe let him drive for a little while.

Uncle Pete jumped out of the car and held out his hand. "Howdy, partner," he said.

Daniel awkwardly shook his uncle's hand. Nobody around here ever shook hands with children; most people didn't even talk to them. Daniel's hand felt like a trapped mouse in his uncle's huge grip. It would sound too childish, Daniel decided, to ask his uncle to take him for a ride.

"Where are your folks?" said Uncle Pete.

"They're out working in the orchard. Want me to ring the dinner bell to call them?"

"Oh, they probably heard the horn. We'll meet at the lunch table," said Uncle Pete. "Have you seen any anthills around here?"

"Lots," said Daniel. "Why?"

"We'll need anthill sand for the trap sites." He picked up a handful of the sandy soil and let it sift between his fingers. "Let's see the traps you found."

"Want to look at my fish first? I put those goldfish you gave me in the cattle tank for the summer."

He led Uncle Pete over to the cowyard. His uncle nodded, but he hardly glanced into the water. He was looking out across the fields.

Daniel felt slighted. He knew that Uncle Pete had hunted whales with the Eskimos on Hudson Bay; maybe he shouldn't expect him to care much about fish in a cattle tank.

But then he saw that Uncle Pete was in a kind of trance. He stood with his hands in his back pockets as his gaze took in everything from the windmill out across the nursery and the cornfield, beyond the creek, past the orchard and the woodlot. He took a deep breath of air, as if to breathe the place into his blood.

Daniel watched him and heard him when he sighed.

"What's the matter, Uncle Pete?"

He put his heavy hand on Daniel's shoulder. "Oh, I get homesick for the place, Danny." Nobody but the vet and Uncle Pete ever called Daniel by a nickname. "I get homesick for you too. Remember when you were a little squirt? You used to ride on my shoulders."

Daniel remembered. In those days, Uncle Pete even helped with the farm work sometimes, and Daniel had tagged behind him everywhere he went, just as Lady tagged along with Daniel.

But now Uncle Pete came only to visit, and when he came, he seemed like a stranger. He had a fancy house in town, but he was rarely there. A magazine sent him all over the world to write about hunting and fishing, and he had made a lot of money, Pa said, on a bass lure he designed.

"You haven't visited since Christmas. Where have you been?"

"Tarpon fishing in Florida," said Uncle Pete. "They fight like the dickens. And I stayed with a trapper in Alaska for a couple of months. We ran his trapline on snowshoes every day."

"Pa wonders why you don't stay around more, if

you like it here." But Daniel knew why. Uncle Pete lived the life Daniel dreamed of for himself.

"Oh, Markham never did understand my itchy feet," said Uncle Pete. "I have to have a change now and then. Besides, I hate all the hard work on a farm. The same work, over and over, day after day, makes me feel like I'm being nibbled to death by ducks."

He took something from his pocket and handed it to Daniel. "Here's something from the Eskimos. It's carved from soapstone."

Daniel looked at the lifelike gray carving of a seal. It was cool, even though it had been in Uncle Pete's pocket, and Daniel noticed that it lay naturally along the curve of his hand when he gripped it. "It feels like the hilt of a knife."

"It looks like one, too, the fleshing knives the hunters use to scrape the fat off seal skins."

Daniel's favorite things were presents Uncle Pete had brought from far places. There was the birchbark box, decorated with brown and white porcupine quills; he kept things like the rattlesnake rattles in that. And the field glasses that Daniel sometimes used to watch the herd of deer across the cornfield. And the wolfskin rug that he kept on his bed. Without

Uncle Pete's presents, his bedroom would have seemed bare.

He felt the seal's cool stone again on his cheek. "You always bring me something wonderful." They thought alike, it seemed. His uncle knew what Daniel needed before Daniel knew himself.

"Now show me the anthills," said Uncle Pete. "And bring a bucket and shovel."

They dug the sand from an anthill by the rockpile where Mama and Daniel had killed the snake.

"A few hills like this, and we'll have enough," said Uncle Pete, as he scooped the sand into the pail. "The ants mix the dirt with their own juices to make this sand. For some reason, it doesn't freeze."

It seemed that Uncle Pete knew everything.

"You have to be smarter than the fox," Uncle Pete went on. "He won't just put his foot in the trap to oblige you. You sprinkle the sand over the trap to hide it. The sand stays loose, so the trap won't freeze up."

Daniel was impressed. Uncle Pete knew how foxes think. "Did you learn that in Alaska?"

"No, that's a homegrown trick. I learned it from my pa when I was a boy."

"Where are you going next?"

"I'm waiting for summer to come in Alaska. A bunch of us are going to fly in to fish for grayling."

"Will you take me with you someday?" Daniel asked.

Uncle Pete smiled. "Let's see how we work together around here before we go traipsing across the world. I'm counting on you to help me with this trapline so I won't have to drive all the way out here every day."

The rest of the afternoon, they cleaned and repaired the fox traps that for years had been hanging among cobwebs in the barn.

Uncle Pete held one in his hand. It was a little longer than his palm. At one end was the spring, a folded strap of metal. Attached to the other end of that spring, a twelve-inch chain hung down. The rusty old trap looked out of place next to Uncle Pete's gold ring. He scratched at the rust with a thumbnail.

"These haven't been used since I was a young man. Your dad never could stomach trapping, and I didn't know much about it then myself," said Uncle Pete.

Daniel saw again in the dusky light of the toolroom how much Pete looked like Pa, but he was even bigger than Pa and taller, louder in his voice and quicker in his movement. Daniel wondered what it meant to "stomach trapping." Pa's words came back. Daniel could help Uncle Pete trap foxes, Pa had said, but "I don't think you're going to like it."

"Your dad would rather plow forty acres than run a trapline once," Uncle Pete said. "It's a wonder he can butcher a chicken."

Uncle Pete rubbed harder on the trap in his hand. "He likes to kneel on bended knee to fiddle with those little trees."

Daniel had never heard anyone criticize Pa before. He glanced at Uncle Pete and fidgeted with the chain on one of the traps. He had seen both Mama and Pa kneel for hours in the tree nursery. He knew what hard work it was to raise fruit trees from seeds.

"We like the trees," said Daniel softly. "People come from miles around to buy our little trees."

Uncle Pete rushed on as if he were deaf to Daniel. "Your folks can't get away overnight. The livestock have to be fed." The heat in his voice surprised Daniel.

His uncle was quiet for a while as he continued to rub the trap. Daniel listened to the ticking of the old school clock Pa kept in the workshop because he liked the sound. Then Uncle Pete went on, quietly now. "Markham belongs here. I don't. Your grandfather tried to force me into farming, but I couldn't wait to escape."

Daniel looked at him sidelong. You like to eat the peaches well enough, he thought.

Uncle Pete stood up abruptly.

"How do you open this thing?" said Daniel, trying to change the subject to one that felt more comfortable. He struggled to force the two sides of the trap apart but couldn't budge them.

"The spring's too heavy for you to open it with just your hands," said Uncle Pete, stepping down on the folded leaf spring at the end. The jaws opened easily then, and he set the trap. Carefully, he placed it flat on the workbench.

"I thought there'd be teeth." Daniel pointed at the smooth edges of the trap's jaws.

"Keep your finger back. If this thing sprang, it could break your bones."

Uncle Pete went into the yard and came back with an oak stick the size of Daniel's finger. "You call this

disk in the middle the 'pan.' That's the trigger." He
touched the pan lightly with the stick. The trap leapt
off the bench with the force of the spring's released
energy, and bit deep into the stick. Its speed and
power reminded Daniel of the striking snake.

"Teeth are for bear traps. They're this big around."

Uncle Pete made a circle with his arms. "Fox legs aren't much bigger than a chicken drumstick. You don't need toothed traps to hold them."

Daniel fingered the crushed stick. "Those foxes won't have a chance, will they?" He tried to sound enthusiastic.

"They won't have a chance if we can trick them into the trap. That's the sport of it. Pitting your own intelligence against the foxes'. Using your knowledge of their habits against them."

Daniel imagined the delicate black leg of a fox in the place of the broken stick and began to wonder whether he would like trapping after all.

Four

After fishing in Alaska, Uncle Pete went to the Rocky Mountains. He showed up once more that summer, in August, between trips, when the early Red Haven peaches were ripe. Daniel was standing on a ladder with his head in a treetop, the same ladder he had climbed all day since dawn.

No one could see whether he was picking or eating or staring into space. The kidney-shaped basket slung around his shoulders was empty. He leaned far out to the side for the biggest peach he could see, one nearly as big as a softball. He smelled its perfume and stroked its velvety cheek on his own. He rubbed the fuzz off on his overalls and bit into the soft fruit. Its sweetness filled him to the toes.

He waved a bee away. "Get your own peach," he said. The fruit was golden, stained rosy red next to the pit. The juice dripped off his chin and ran down his arm, leaving white streaks on his dusty skin. He dropped the pit on Lady, who was sleeping on her side under the ladder; she jumped as if shot.

Daniel could hear the hired pickers talking quietly to one another through the treetops. At the end of the aisle between the trees, he saw Mama driving the sputtering tractor back into the orchard, returning the wagon for another load. Uncle Pete stood behind her, hanging on to the tractor's fender.

Pa had not only organized the pickers and picked more peaches than anyone else, but he also loaded the wagon. Now he reached up and squeezed Daniel's ankle as he waited for Mama to drive up the aisle.

"How you doing?" Pa asked, with a dazzling smile on his face. He picked up a crate of peaches and hoisted it onto the wagon before it had stopped. Daniel jumped the last few ladder rungs.

"Look what the cat dragged in," said Mama, as Uncle Pete swung down from the tractor fender and rumpled Daniel's hair.

"I'm glad you're home again," said Pa, shaking hands with his brother.

"It's been a long summer," said Uncle Pete. "I couldn't wait to unpack my gear so I could drive out to see you."

"Well," Pa said, with an edge on his voice, "we can always use an extra hand at harvest."

"I'm sure of that," said Uncle Pete with a toss of his head. "But I wasn't offering my services as a hired hand."

Pa clapped the dust off his hands and wiped them on the bib of his overalls. He cleared his throat, as if to start the conversation over again. "Sorry I bristled," he said. "How were the Rockies?"

"Same as ever," said Uncle Pete. "I got chased by a grizzly. How's the farm?"

"Same as ever," said Pa. "I got chased by the chickens."

They laughed, but Pa went on loading the crates of peaches. Uncle Pete helped for a while and then stood by with his hands in his hip pockets. His plaid shirt looked new; it had a canvas recoil pad stitched to the shoulder where a shotgun stock would rest.

"Have you been collecting the ant sand?" he asked.

"I've found bushels of it," said Daniel. "When can we start?"

"Not until cold weather."

Daniel kicked a stone in disappointment.

"We could start right now if all we wanted was the bounty," said Uncle Pete. "But I'd rather wait until the fur is prime, when the foxes have grown their winter coats."

Daniel saw Pa nod in agreement.

"They're beautiful animals," Uncle Pete said. "I'd hate to waste the fur."

Uncle Pete didn't stay for dinner, and he didn't come back until harvest was over, in early October. He was writing a book about the Rockies, he said. Although he didn't like farm work, Uncle Pete worked hard, Daniel noticed. But traveling and writing about the mountains seemed like an odd kind of work.

By October, Daniel was sick at the thought of peaches. He had peeled three bushels that his mother canned, and another bushel for jam. And he thought he had picked at least a ton. Even after school started in September, he was on a ladder at dawn and went

back to the ladder when he came home, and worked until sunset.

Pa was always smiling or whistling "Alice Blue Gown," his favorite song, while he picked. But Daniel began to wish he'd never seen a peach. Every year, his parents expected him to work a little harder with the harvest. The arches of his feet were sore where the ladder rungs pressed. His shoulders ached from the strap of the loaded picking basket. Juice had stained his hands a brown that soap couldn't fade.

He would stand at the top of the eight-foot ladder dreaming about trapping foxes with Uncle Pete. Or else he imagined himself fishing with the neighborhood kids down on the Black River, or catching frogs in the creek. But all the other kids in the township had brown hands too; Daniel knew that their heads were in the treetops of their own families' orchards.

When no one was looking, Daniel often came down from the ladder to romp with Lady. She had grown more friendly and playful over the summer. If Daniel tossed a ripe peach her way, she chomped it in midair and gobbled it, drizzling juice from her chin. Still he worried. She had run away once; it could happen again.

In the midst of the harvest, Daniel's family spen several days budding the seedling trees in the nursery. This was the time of year when the transplanted buds would "take," when they would grow on a new tree. As soon as light dawned, the Beckman family were on their hands and knees.

"Now watch us bud a few," said Pa, "and then you try one."

Daniel knelt between his parents, watching their nimble hands. Lady sat behind him, watching over his shoulder. With the steel blades of their jackknives, Mama and Pa made little vertical slits in the bark of the young trees they had grown from last year's peach pits. They were hardly more than sticks with a plume of leaves.

"You cut just through the bark, like this," said Pa, "then make another cut across that first one. Now you turn your knife around." He opened the ivory blade and showed Daniel that its edge wouldn't cut skin. "The ivory is flexible; it slips easily in the sap under the bark."

He worked steadily as he talked. "These are Red Haven buds, so a Red Haven sprout will grow on this seedling." Under the loosened corners of the cut cross, he slipped a bud he had slivered from a hybrid orchard tree.

"Why do all this work?" said Daniel. "Why not just plant Red Haven peach pits in the first place?"

"Hybrids don't grow true from their seeds," said Mama. "You'd get a peach of some kind, but it wouldn't have the outstanding traits of the Red Haven. You want that beautiful red cheek, and the large size, and the delicious sweet juice." As she talked, she bound the bud in place with rubber bands. "These will stretch as the tree grows."

"And after the bud takes, and starts to grow," said Pa, "we'll clip off the original wood above the graft. The new trunk will produce bigger, juicier, tastier peaches than would have grown on the natural seedling."

Daniel looked down the row of little trees, then across to the next row, and the next, and the one after that. "There must be a hundred trees here," he said. "My back aches already."

"Three hundred," said Mama. "This is next year's bread and butter."

The sun was hot on Daniel's neck, and his knees

felt stiff from kneeling. He was afraid of this new job. He might cut too deep; the knife might slip and cut off the tender top of the seedling. Besides, he thought, if I learn how to do it, this will be my job for the rest of my life.

"Want to try one?" said Pa.

"I'd rather pick," said Daniel. He saw his parents exchange a glance. They wanted him to be exactly like them. But Daniel had itchy feet like Uncle Pete. He didn't want to be tied to a farm for the rest of his life.

At the top of a ladder, hidden from the other pickers among the leaves, Daniel could find ways to play, and nobody would know. So he spent the rest of the day in the orchard, dreaming and staring out across the river, thinking of Uncle Pete's green car and gold ring. He was waiting for winter, when the trapping would begin.

Five

When the peach harvest was over, Pa said, "Let's rest for a few days before the corn crew comes." The crew traveled around the countryside with expensive machinery to harvest the corn and chop the stalks for cattle fodder.

So Daniel and his parents "rested," picking the purple Concord grapes and canning juice, cutting and stacking firewood, repairing the wagon, shoveling out the chicken coop, feeding and milking the cows, preparing the buildings for winter, cleaning up the garden, and storing the last of the vegetables. Four Hubbard squash were so big they had to be carted in the wheelbarrow.

Some rest, thought Daniel.

Whatever Daniel did, Lady was always underfoot. Still, he didn't trust her; sometimes he dreamed that she had run away again.

One Saturday in October, Uncle Pete drove in at midmorning, when Daniel and Pa were fixing the barnyard fence. Daniel waved and waited for Pa to tell him he could quit work now.

"You remind me of that dog, the way you wag your tail when Pete comes around," said Pa.

A goldfish surfaced in the cattle tank, a flash of brilliance in the dark water.

"It's time to take those fish in, Daniel," said Pa. "There was a skin of ice on the tank this morning."

"Okay," said Daniel, but he danced away to Uncle Pete. "Is it cold enough yet? Did you come to lay the trapline?"

Pa and Uncle Pete nodded hello. As always, there seemed to be some secret obstacle between them. Daniel thought it might be the deep disagreement in the ways they chose to live.

"No, today we're only going to cook the traps."

In the trunk of the car were two deep baskets, woven of split wood, with shoulder straps. "Don't handle them," said Uncle Pete when Daniel reached; "not unless you're wearing gloves like these."

As Uncle Pete put horsehide gloves on his well-groomed hands, Daniel glimpsed the gold ring that he coveted. Then he caught a whiff of the gloves. "Pee-you!" he said.

Uncle Pete smiled. "They're smeared with fox urine and scent from glands on the foxes' feet," he said. "You can buy little bottles of the stuff from suppliers or collect it from the animals you trap. It covers up the man smell."

"You've learned a lot since we were boys," said Pa. "Then we just set the traps on the bare ground."

"There was more game in those days."

"Yes," said Pa. "Remember when we could just drop a line into the Black and come up with a fish?"

Uncle Pete nodded. "I've been talking to the old trappers who make a living on furs. It isn't easy to outsmart foxes anywhere, especially in country like this, where they're wary of people."

"Pa?" Daniel turned to Pa, silently asking permission to help Uncle Pete.

"We've the stock to tend, Daniel. And I want to look over the nursery trees with you."

"I can learn the chores anytime," said Daniel, "but Uncle Pete hardly ever comes."

You want me to be your hired hand, Daniel thought, with a ring in my nose. You're afraid I'll grow up and leave the farm, like Uncle Pete. He glanced at his uncle, who was keeping his mouth shut and looking out across the fields.

It almost seemed that Pa had heard Daniel's thoughts. His nostrils flared as they always did when he disapproved but wasn't saying so. "All right, Daniel. You have choices of your own to make. Trapping it is. I'll finish the fence."

Uncle Pete slung one packbasket on his back, and Daniel imitated him. They walked down the road to the gully where the sumac grew. Daniel followed his uncle's lead, picking big bunches of the dark red sumac berries until the baskets were nearly full.

Lady rushed around sniffing the grass. Daniel had realized by now that her main worry was not figuring out a plan to run away again, but keeping sight of Daniel.

"Are these berries the bait?" Daniel pointed at the basket.

"Keep your eyes open, and you'll see."

Back at the house, Mama silently got out the big blue canning kettle when Uncle Pete asked for it.

"I'll let you use my kettle," she said, allowing the screen door to slam behind her, "but I don't have to like it."

"She doesn't have the stomach for trapping either," said Uncle Pete.

Daniel wondered what Uncle Pete could be planning to do with the kettle. What was so bad that it would make his mother rude? He hurried toward the barn with Uncle Pete.

"Having the stomach" meant being brave enough somehow, Daniel decided. He wondered whether he had it. If he had the stomach, maybe he could live an exciting life. He could hunt polar bears in the Arctic waste like Uncle Pete. He could fish for tarpon in Florida.

They cooked the sumac berries on the hotplate in the toolshed until the water was thick and black and the air was heavy with a spicy acrid odor. Then they cooked the traps in several batches. The smell drove Lady out into the yard.

"You look like a witch stirring that pot," said Daniel.

Uncle Pete snorted. Then he answered Daniel's earlier question in his roundabout way. "This is not the bait, as you can see. You know what foxes eat; they're not vegetarians, my boy. This stuff stains the metal and covers up our smell. And the sumac oil greases the moving parts."

Daniel felt embarrassed. He knew of course that foxes eat small animals; he had been a farm boy all his life. But he had thought that Uncle Pete might know something more.

When the traps had dried, Uncle Pete put them in the packbasket and stowed it under the workbench. He dusted his gloved hands together, as if to end the job. "Now we're all ready."

"When?"

"December."

Daniel went to bed that night troubled by the feeling that he had forgotten to do something. Lady thumped her tail a few thumps under his bed as he scratched her ears. Then Daniel drifted off to sleep and dreams of trapping with Uncle Pete.

That night a hard frost killed all the flowers and vegetable plants in the garden and froze a solid sheet of ice on the cattle tank.

In the morning, the sun melted the ice. Daniel found the goldfish floating on the surface of the dark water, their orange color faded, their flashing brilliance dulled.

It's time to take those fish in, Pa had said.

Daniel looked up and found that Pa was watching him. "I forgot."

Pa turned his back and walked away.

Daniel wrapped the dead fish in a clean wisp of hay and climbed the oak tree. There was a hole in the trunk. In that hole, where he had buried a bird the cats had killed and a kitten that the cows had stepped on, Daniel laid the fish.

In silence, with sober thoughts, he worked double labor all that day.

Six

The night before Uncle Pete came to lay the trapline, Daniel couldn't sleep. He saw himself in the Alaska bush, living in a cabin he had built alone. He would shoot a moose each year and hang the meat high in a tree to keep it from the wolverines. He would trap all winter, doing the things Uncle Pete's articles advised—carrying matches coated with wax to keep them dry; avoiding the outside of a bend in a stream, where fast water makes the ice treacherous. His only livestock would be Lady. They would both sleep late every day.

But Uncle Pete rousted him out of bed in the morning even before Pa was awake. Daniel shut Lady in the house to keep her out of the traps, and then ran across the yard to catch up with Uncle Pete.

"Can't we drive?" said Daniel, thinking of the smooth comfort of the green car and the smell of its leather when the heater was on.

"I don't want to carry fox carcasses around in my car," said Uncle Pete. "We may as well get used to the hike now, when we have only traps to pack." He heaved the heavy pack, filled with the steel traps and other supplies, onto his own shoulders. Daniel shouldered the lighter one, which Uncle Pete had already loaded with the forked stakes standing on end inside it.

When they reached the tree nursery, Uncle Pete looked at the graft on one of the young trees. "Your dad's attached to his life in a way I'll never be," he said. "He's more like the Eskimos than I am."

Daniel thought of the Eskimos hunting whales in an Arctic bay, and tried to imagine Pa in their boat. Pa didn't look right with a harpoon in his hand. "What do you mean about the Eskimos?"

"They're tied to their country the way Markham is to this farm. They don't get restless the way I do and run across the world looking for something new."

Uncle Pete was full of surprises, Daniel thought. First he had criticized Pa's life; now he praised it. Daniel's parents never talked of such things. They just did their work.

"Your dad has you besides. I envy him that." Uncle Pete touched Daniel's shoulder as they went on their way.

They watched the sun come up as they walked for miles through light snow before they set the first trap. Uncle Pete chose a hillock for the site; he said that foxes like to look around the countryside and watch for game.

"We'll set ten traps, each one closer to home," said Uncle Pete. "That's the trapline. When we finish up, we'll be within smelling distance of breakfast."

"What's the bait?" said Daniel. "You never did answer my question. What's to lure them?"

"Don't get ahead of yourself, squirt," said Uncle Pete, smiling.

With a sledgehammer, he pounded a forked stake into the ground, through the big ring at the end of the trap's chain. He poured out a little ant sand and placed the trap open on top, and then sprinkled more sand over the jaws of the trap. From the bottom of Daniel's packbasket, he took a piece of gray fur in his gloved hand. He rubbed it on the sand near the trap and dropped it a few feet away, where it made a small thud.

It was not just a piece of fur, Daniel saw. "A kitten," he said.

"Not a kitten, Daniel. Bait." Uncle Pete looked up with a wry smile. "Try as I may, I can't lure foxes without bait."

Daniel thought of the gray tabby that lived in the feedroom and the five kittens that were just beginning to leave her side. "Not ours . . . ?"

"No, your pa wouldn't let me have any of yours. I had to go to Brenners' and a couple of other places." Uncle Pete looked at Daniel. "What did you expect, son, a piece of cheese? Sumac berries?"

Daniel did not reply. But he looked around for Lady automatically, before he remembered that she was safe at home.

Uncle Pete touched Daniel's cheek with his fingers, near enough to his nose so Daniel could smell the fox scent on the gloves. "Just between you and me, I get

less kick out of things like this every year. Shall we stop?"

"No!" said Daniel. "I can take it!"

"Did you watch carefully so you can set the next one?"

Daniel nodded, but his excitement had blown away in the cold wind that swept the fields.

Nevertheless he followed, trying to step in Uncle Pete's footprints, fingering the snake's rattle that he carried in his pocket as a reminder of the time he had been brave.

Wearing his own leather gloves, he prepared the next site. Uncle Pete showed him how to open the jaws of the trap with his hands, while he stepped on the spring.

"You can't run the trapline every morning on your own unless you're strong enough to reset the traps. And careful enough so you don't trap yourself," said Uncle Pete. "Can you handle it?"

"Of course I can handle it," said Daniel. He wondered whether Pa had been telling Uncle Pete that Daniel was irresponsible. He would show them both, he thought.

When he had driven the stake and laid the trap and sprinkled the sand, Daniel put his hands in his pockets, fidgeting with the rattle through the glove leather.

"The bait, Daniel."

"You show me one more time. I didn't see what you did with the last one."

Uncle Pete brought another kitten from the bottom of the basket, a yellow one this time. Its eyes were closed. Daniel turned his back and looked across the fields toward the orchards of home.

"Watch what I do, Daniel. The next one is yours." Uncle Pete dropped the kitten. "If you can't stomach the bait, how will you live with a fox in the trap?"

"I can do it. I'll do the next one," said Daniel in a rush. "Show me how again."

He forced himself to watch. And at the next site, he drove the stake, laid the trap, sprinkled the sand, and placed the bait himself.

The kitten was black this time, black with white paws.

Seven

Uncle Pete checked the ten traps alone the next morning, but Daniel ran the line with him again after school.

As they approached each trap, Daniel felt drawn to it. His excitement drowned out his other feelings; it was loud music overwhelming birdsong. He would stretch his body and strain his eyes, trying to see over hills and around fencerow brush, hoping for the first glimpse of the first fox they would catch. By now, he had memorized the route.

Near one trap, Uncle Pete showed him tracks circling the area. "Are you sure they aren't dog tracks?" asked Daniel, remembering that dogs and foxes belonged to the same family.

"No. Not for certain. Except these are the right size for a fox," said Uncle Pete. "This one may have caught a hint of our scent. He's cautious."

They walked on toward the next trap. "Be sure to keep Lady locked up, by the way," Uncle Pete said.

Daniel pushed thoughts of Lady out of his mind, unable to stand the idea of hurting his own dog. Such thoughts spoiled his excitement. But once again every trap was empty, with the bait untouched.

On the second day, Daniel thought he was going to be disappointed again. There had been nothing in the traps that morning, and nothing so far this afternoon. But as they approached the last trap, back on Daniel's own farm, at the crest of a hill, he saw that the snow was scuffed away in a perfect circle. The fox huddled in a shallow dip it had scratched in the sandy soil, blending in, one color with another, all copper and white.

Daniel ran ahead until his uncle's shouted warning stopped him. "He'll bite!"

Uncle Pete overtook Daniel. Watching them both with burning golden eyes, the fox leapt away to the far side of the circle it had scratched in the ground

with its struggle. It pulled against the trap that held
its black front foot, and the trap pulled against the
short chain, which the stake held fast. The fox fought
against the trap, snarling, with its lips curled back,
biting at its own foot.

"Steady," said Uncle Pete. He quietly set the basket
down and drew an extra stake out of it, his eyes holding the fox's fiery gaze. He approached the animal and
rapped it sharply on the nose with the heavy stake.
The fox dropped where it stood.

Daniel's heart was racing. "Is he dead?"

"Not yet." Uncle Pete turned the animal on its side and then stepped on its rib cage.

"What are you doing?" said Daniel. "You'll hurt him!"

"He'll suffocate," said Uncle Pete, panting to catch his breath. "This way, we kill him without his suffering anymore and without damaging the fur."

Uncle Pete stood with both feet and all of his weight on the unconscious fox's body. He stood there until Daniel thought a lifetime had passed. He could hear his heart pounding in his head, but he could not think; the sight of Uncle Pete standing on the fox filled his mind, pushing everything else aside.

Uncle Pete stepped down at last and made sure that the fox was dead. "He's a beaut," he said, touching the fox's ear with his gloved fingers. "It's a pity."

He sighed, and Daniel thought Uncle Pete might be sorry for what he had done. But he turned his back abruptly on Daniel and the fox. "Put him in the pack," he said. "I'll reset this trap."

The fox lay at Daniel's feet. A moment before, taut with desperate vitality, it had seemed enormous. Now it was only a pile of rusty, furry rags, much smaller than Lady. Daniel had never been so near a fox before. He saw the delicate black nose and muzzle, the black-tipped ears, the four black legs and feet, one of them torn almost off.

"After supper," said Uncle Pete, "I'll show you how to skin him out."

Daniel was afraid he was going to throw up. He knelt beside the fox and stroked its white neck. He looked into its dainty face, hoping it would bound away and go home to its brothers and lick its foot until it healed. Daniel saw its dog's tongue. Fine black whiskers stitched its muzzle. But the fox did not stir.

His own arms and legs felt almost too heavy to move, but he picked up the fox. It flopped over his arms, but the wind lifted its brush of a tail and ruffled its fur in a counterfeit imitation of life. Daniel placed it as gently as he could in the basket.

Then he turned away from Uncle Pete, who had smoothed the mound and reset the trap and was scattering the ant sand over it. Daniel began to walk away.

"Daniel?" Uncle Pete called. "Partner?"

Daniel didn't say a word. He kept on walking, straight across the field, toward the orchard and home.

All the way, he thought he heard Uncle Pete's voice, wistful and sad, in the birdcalls and the sound of the wind. "Daniel? Partner?"

Eight

The dusk was already gathering when Daniel cut through the orchard. The trees were bare, but he comforted himself by remembering drifts of pink petals on his shoulders. The nursery was only a regiment of bare sticks now, but he saw them leafy green in springtime. As he passed the chicken coop, he could hear the hens muttering inside as hens do when they sit on eggs.

Daniel was trotting now, thinking of Lady and her foxlike legs and feet. She might have gotten out and followed him. His trail would have led her straight to the traps.

He was calling her name as he rushed through the back porch and burst into the lighted kitchen, where

Mama was putting a meat loaf and baking potatoes into the oven.

Lady bounded into the kitchen and greeted him so wildly she nearly knocked him down. She put her front feet on his shoulders and licked his face and ears and neck, with special attention to his ears. Captain used to greet him like that, back in the happy days.

"That dog," said Mama. "She sat looking out this back window with her chin on the ledge all the time you were gone, moaning and whining and carrying on like a widow lady."

Laughing, drowning in Lady's spitbath, Daniel knelt down and put his cold face in her warm neck. "You're my dog now," he said, and he knew that she would never run away again. Relief washed over Daniel; Lady was safe, and she loved him.

"What did you find in those foul traps?" asked Mama.

"Not much." Daniel hated questions. When he was upset about something, he wanted time to sort out his feelings for himself.

Mama turned the searchlight on him, that measuring, mind-reading gaze of hers that wouldn't let any secret lie buried. The canary by the window stopped singing. "Where's Pete?" asked Mama.

"He'll be along." Daniel clattered upstairs to his room, still wearing his parka. Lady curled up on the bed beside him and lay still, letting him look at the design of her paw. He had never cared before how spongy the pads were, or how the foot splayed out to distribute weight. Inside her foot, he could feel little chains of jointed bones like his finger. They were connected to other bones like his hand, and even to something like his wrist.

A door slammed below. The smell of meat loaf and potatoes floated up the stairs on the music of Pa's deep voice mixed with Uncle Pete's. Hungry though he was, Daniel ignored Mama's call for supper and pretended to be sleeping when she came to get him. He felt her taking off his shoes and covering him with a quilt. He felt her cool hand on his forehead, checking for a fever. She shut his door quietly and tiptoed down the stairs.

Uncle Pete was going to show him how to skin a fox after supper. You pulled the skin down like a glove, Uncle Pete had said once, so you wouldn't

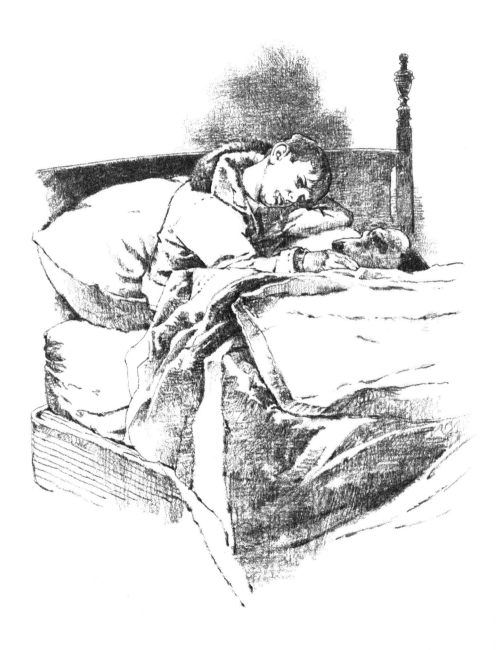

damage the pelt. Daniel dozed off, stroking the wolf-skin on his bed and thinking of a goldfish flashing in the sun. He dreamed he was standing in the top of a tree, crowing to the world. Foxes played below him among the young trees in the nursery. He and Uncle Pete caught a whale in the pond on hook and line.

Daniel was up before the roosters in the morning. With Lady sticking like a shadow, he ate a thick slab of Mama's bread as he fed and watered the cows. Shutting the door to the feedroom, he bumped into something damp, hanging on a nail. The foxskin was turned inside out, stretched on a steel frame, scraped clean of fat, and hung to dry. The bushy tail, stripped off the bone, hung limp.

Daniel knocked over an old three-legged milking stool. Lady jumped, and the cows shifted noisily in their stanchions.

Pa always said that it was Daniel's duty to remember the creatures that depended on him. He could not go on trapping foxes. Yet he couldn't bear to tell Uncle Pete that he was quitting.

He reached for the electric lantern that hung on a nail by the door and took a stake from Uncle Pete's packbasket. The barn door squeaked on its runners as he rolled it shut. Needs grease, he thought. I'll do that when I come back.

"Come on, Lady," he said. "We've got a trapline to run."

The kitchen light switched on as they passed the chicken coop. Mama would be setting the coffeepot on the stove, and Pa would be pulling on his barn boots.

Daniel could see no stars in the cloudy sky, no lights ahead as he left the soft glow of the yard behind and passed the rockpile where he and Mama had killed the snake. He could smell snow on the cold, blustery wind. If they didn't move the rocks soon, they would have to wait for spring. He hoped that the snakes had sense enough to hibernate now so he wouldn't step on one in the dark.

Although the fields and orchards and woodlots of all the surrounding farms had always been Daniel's playground, he never left the farmyard alone at night. He was afraid of the dark. But now Lady was his bodyguard. He kept his bearings by following the straight lines of the lane and then the orchard.

He turned right at the first fencerow and followed that to an intersecting fence. He crossed the creek where he had found a pocketful of crayfish claws the day Lady ran away. There were the Osage orange trees where he collected the hard pebbly fruit every autumn to use as balls at school. There was the black-walnut tree where Mama picked nuts for her delicious cakes. He saw the layout of the neighboring farms in his mind as if it were a map.

They took the two-rut road through the woods where Lady once had fled. Somewhere too near, a big owl hooted, like a sentry demanding the password. With a shiver, Daniel put the stake he had brought under his arm and reached out for Lady, gripping her collar for protection.

The sky had still been dark when they entered the woods, but as they left it, first light was breaking. Daniel crossed Brenners' back field and cut through Gallos' orchard. Before he and Lady reached the far-thest trap, Daniel had switched the lantern off. He knew the exact location of every site. Well before they reached the first one, he gripped Lady's collar again. Now he was her bodyguard, so she couldn't run away and be caught, lured by Uncle Pete's bait.

Cutting across the field, Daniel went straight to the trap, trembling for fear there might be something in it. But as he approached, he saw that it was empty. He jabbed at the trigger with the stake and missed. He touched the pan gently with the point of the stake. Faster than he could see, the jaws sprang shut on the wood. He struggled to pry them open enough to release the stake.

The next five traps were empty too. Daniel sprang them all with little sticks or pebbles. The snow was worn away in a circle around the seventh, and the earth was deeply scratched. Daniel found a delicate black foot still caught in the sprung trap, but the fox was gone. He felt the spongy pads, and the little chains of delicate bones, and moved the claws with his finger. The blood was dried. Gently he put the foot in his pocket, and then he kicked the trap across the mound to the end of its chain.

"We'll run your trapline for you, Uncle Pete!" he shouted, but his voice sounded thin on the wind. For a moment, he saw himself, asking Uncle Pete to teach him how to trap. He remembered that his letters to his uncle had come close to begging. This trapline belonged to Daniel too; how could he stop now? He stuffed the memories down deep, letting the anger rise again.

He yanked on the chain and pried at the stake that pinned the trap, but couldn't draw the rough wood out of the ground. With Lady romping at his side, he trotted the rest of the route, breathless with fear that another animal might be caught while he tarried. When he had sprung the final trap, where yesterday's fox had died, he threw the stake he had carried end over end as far as he could. Yesterday's fox hung in the barn today, a scrap of fur.

All the way home Daniel tried to think of a plausible story to tell. His explanation would have to be good; Uncle Pete was no dumbbell. Nearing the yard, Daniel saw the green car pulled up near the porch. He knew at once that he had been kidding himself. When Uncle Pete found the traps sprung, he would not be fooled, no matter what Daniel said.

Nine

"Where in the world have you been?" said Pa when Daniel dragged into the barn, miserable with the thought that Uncle Pete would know he had sabotaged the traps. "Last night we thought you were sick. This morning, when we looked in your room, you had disappeared. What's going on, Daniel?"

"I couldn't sleep, so I took Lady for a walk."

"Before the cows were milked? Before breakfast? For an hour and a half?" Pa went on pouring a white stream of milk into tall cans that the truck would pick up.

Daniel put his hands in his pockets. His left hand fingered the finely jointed rattle of the snake, while the right stroked the fox's foot. "I just wanted to see the sunrise."

"What happened yesterday with Uncle Pete?"

"Nothing much. He caught a fox."

"So I saw," said Pa, nodding in the direction of the skin. "He said he didn't think you liked trapping much."

"Well, I went out to check the traps for him this morning!"

Daniel heard the lie he was telling and felt guilty. Lady rubbed against his leg, as if to tell him she loved him anyway.

"Oh, yes?"

Daniel hated that know-it-all tone of voice Pa had. "No luck." He turned away so Pa couldn't read his feelings in his face. "What's Uncle Pete doing here so early?"

"Waiting for you, Daniel." Pa put his arm around Daniel's shoulders. "Let's see if we can scare up some breakfast. The schoolbus already left anyway."

Daniel groaned. "Did it come early, or am I that late?"

"Never mind. Some things that have to be learned you don't necessarily learn at school."

Daniel's thoughts were jumbled. If Uncle Pete knew,

then Pa knew too. But he had already lied to Pa. If Pa knew, then he also knew that Daniel had lied. Yet Pa didn't seem angry. If he didn't know, Daniel would have to keep on lying to prevent his finding out.

Daniel rubbed his eyes with the heel of his hand, trying to cover up the tears.

"What happened out there, son?" said Pa quietly.

Daniel looked defiantly at his father. "This happened!" He handed Pa the black fox's foot. "I can't stand it, Pa."

"Did you think you'd have to convince me? Do you think you'll have to convince Pete? We'll go up to the house now and talk to him about it." To Daniel's surprise, Pa's voice was soft. "There are all kinds of courage, Daniel." He gave Daniel an easy nudge. "Come on. You've got to face it sometime."

Lady raced them to the house and won.

"Well, here's our big eater," said Mama in the kitchen. She put a pan of biscuits in the oven, as if she had been waiting for Daniel to come.

"What are you doing here, Uncle Pete?" he asked.

"I thought you might have forgotten who talked who into trapping, Daniel. I thought we might talk it over."

Pa put the fox's foot in the middle of the wooden kitchen table, right between the butter dish and the bowl of jam.

Uncle Pete glanced at it and then looked at Daniel's face. "I see you've been checking our traps."

Daniel hung his parka on a peg. The drab coats and jackets were lined up limp on the wall like so many cast-off skins. He leaned his forehead against the cold plaster, wishing the canary would be still.

"I sprang 'em all, Uncle Pete," he said to the wall.

"Well, good. There's no hurry then, is there? They can't do any harm while we take our time with breakfast."

Daniel turned to look at him. Uncle Pete was studying the fox's foot just as Daniel had studied Lady's the night before.

His eyes met Daniel's. "The older I get, the more this kind of suffering bothers me." He weighed the foot in his hand. "I can't stomach trapping anymore myself. I was going to get you out of bed this morning and talk you into pulling the traps, but . . ."

". . . I beat you to it," Daniel said. He gave his uncle a long look. "What about the chicken coops the foxes were raiding?"

"Humph. Pa was mainly exaggerating," said Mama. "Any farmer who's worth a nickel can keep foxes out of the chicken coop." She transferred the hot biscuits into bowls one at a time, so quickly that her bare hand scarcely touched them.

"What about the pheasants?" asked Daniel.

"The foxes will die off because they don't have enough pheasants to eat," said Pa. "Then the pheasants will come back. Then there will be more foxes to cut back the pheasant population."

"When this is dry," said Uncle Pete, gesturing with the black foot, "you can put a ring on it, like a rabbit foot, and keep it for a souvenir of the time your uncle tried to make a trapper out of a farmer."

"No," said Daniel, taking the foot from his uncle's hand and wrapping it in a napkin. "I won't need a trophy." The fox's foot belonged in the dark hole at the heart of the oak, not dangling like some gimcrack from a keyring. The snake rattle might belong there too.

Mama put a knob of butter on each of the big biscuits and spooned stewed peaches over their tops. "Your favorite, Daniel. Hot peach shortcake."

"What do you say we raise some pheasant chicks next spring?" said Uncle Pete. "We don't have to give up being partners just because we decided to quit trapping." He glanced at Pa. "I'd like to spend more time out here anyway. Make myself useful."

Daniel imagined himself at the helm of a fast boat with Uncle Pete, flying across the water in the Florida sun. That was what he had given up. And he thought of all the dull days ahead when, instead of adventuring, he would be shoveling manure out of the chicken coop.

"I guess I'll never get to travel now," he said.

Mama touched Daniel's cheek. "Farming wouldn't have to be all or nothing, the way we do it," she said.

Lady put her head in Daniel's lap.

"You don't have to go to such extremes, Daniel," Uncle Pete burst out. "Adventures don't always end in killing. Besides, hunting and fishing aren't necessarily as cruel as leg-hold traps."

Daniel and Pa held each other's gaze as Uncle Pete went on, each watching the other's reaction. "Maybe your folks could spare you next June. You and I could light out for the mountains. And when harvest comes, maybe I could help around here."

"I don't have to go to extremes," Daniel told his father, turning Uncle Pete's phrase over in his mind as he spoke. "I'd like to learn to bud the trees."

Pa smiled at Daniel with the same pleasure he poured out to a sunset or an oriole's trill. "I think we could spare you in June," he said.

Daniel and Pa shook hands across the table to seal their promise to each other. Everybody laughed, as people do when a storm breaks and turns into a gentle rain.

Daniel realized that he was starved. Mama served him three venison sausages and poured a tall glass of buttermilk from the pitcher with the blue cat on the front. As he dug into his food, Daniel slipped one of the sausages to Lady under the table. He saw that Mama saw, but this time she didn't scold.

"The deer meat tastes good," said Uncle Pete.

"Last season we got one of those big bucks that had been eating my corn," said Pa.

But for Daniel, the earlier conversation wasn't over. "I might raise peaches when I grow up," he said. "Or maybe apples. I like apples."

Stroking Lady's silky ears, he looked out the window and across the farm.

Beyond the windmill and the barn, snow was falling now on the shoulders of the peach trees and covering the scratched earth by the seventh trap. But in his mind, Daniel saw a cloud of petals in the air and heard the buzz of bees.